W9-AVR-379

1991

Triffic

the Extraordinary Pig

by **DICK KING-SMITH**

author of *Babe: The Gallant Pig*

illustrated by Cary Pillo

Text copyright © 1991 by Foxbusters Ltd.

Illustrations copyright © 1998 by Troll Communications L.L.C.

Planet Reader is a trademark of Troll Communications L.L.C.

Published by Troll Communications L.L.C.

All rights reserved. No part of this book may be reproduced or utilized in any form or by any means, electronic or mechanical, including photocopying, recording, or by any information storage and retrieval system, without written permission from the publisher.

First published in Great Britain in *Dick King-Smith's Triffic Pig Book* by Victor Gollancz Ltd. 1991.
This edition first published by Victor Gollancz 1994.
Published in Puffin Books 1998.
First Troll edition published 1998 by arrangement with Penguin Books Ltd.

Printed in the United States of America.

10 9 8 7 6 5 4 3 2 1

Contents

Chapter 1

Only One Girl

"Only one girl?" cried Mrs. Berkshire in tones of horror.

"I'm afraid so," answered the unhappy voice of Mrs. Tamworth. "The other five are all boys."

"Oh, I am sorry!" said Mrs. Berkshire.

For a moment longer she stood with her front feet resting on top of the wall that separated their two sties. She stared into the dark interior where mother and children lay. Then Mrs. Berkshire heaved her bulk back down and called to her neighbor on the other side, Mrs. Gloucester Old-Spots.

"Glossy!"

"What is it, Betty?" came the reply.

"Teresa Tamworth has had her babies."

"All is well, I hope? How many piglets did she have?"

"Six. But there's only one girl."

"Oh, dear. Oh, dear!" grunted Mrs. Old-Spots, and she hurried, Betty Berkshire could hear, to pass this disturbing piece of news on down the line of pigsties. In just a few minutes, Molly Middle-White, Sarah Saddleback, and Laetitia Large-Black all knew that poor Teresa Tamworth's litter contained—sad to say—only one girl.

"What a pity!" they exclaimed. And there was much tut-tutting and shaking of heavy

heads as the five other sows at the Rare Breeds Survival Center discussed (in low voices) the Tamworth tragedy. A common pig on an ordinary farm might not care at all about the gender of her newborn children, but for a sow of a Rare Breed it was a very different matter.

Mrs. Tamworth's male piglets, the little hogs, were destined merely for the butcher. But their sister, the gilt, the little female, was precious beyond belief. In time she would become a mother herself. She would help increase the number of her kind, making her particular Rare Breed that much less rare.

This was true of all the animals in the Survival Center: the cows hoped desperately

for heifer calves, the sheep for ewe lambs, the mares for filly foals, and the hens for pullets. If lots of female babies were born, their breeds would live on. If not, these breeds would disappear—a fate that had already overtaken so many of the old breeds of British livestock.

But Teresa Tamworth had had only one girl!

"Her first litter, I believe," said Laetitia Large-Black to Sarah Saddleback. Laetitia and Sarah were both experienced mothers. "Let's hope she doesn't overlay any of them."

"Especially the girl," agreed Sarah. "That would be awful."

Molly Middle-White grunted in sympathy, but she could not keep a look of smug satisfaction off her squashed-in face. She was nursing a litter of eight, of which six were female.

Meanwhile, back in her sty, Teresa lay deep in straw and thought, suckling her six baby Tamworths. Sandy red in color like their mother, they nuzzled greedily at her. None was more determined than the solitary girl, who was already shoving her brothers out of the way. Their hunger at last satisfied, the piglets slept, and Teresa got carefully to her feet.

Betty Berkshire's head appeared over the wall.

"Is everything all right, dear?" she asked.

"Yes," said Teresa. She sighed deeply. "If only they all could have been girls," she said.

"Now, now," Betty answered briskly. "You mustn't worry. It could happen to any sow."

Teresa needs something to take her mind off her troubles, she said to herself. *I know— choosing names. That's a nice diversion.*

"What are you going to call them?" Betty asked.

"I hadn't thought about it," said Teresa.

"Not that it matters much what you choose for the boys—Tom, Dick, or Harry, any old name will do," said Betty. "In fact, I wouldn't bother naming them if I were you. But the girl, now that's different. Especially because she's the only one. It would be nice to call her something out of the ordinary, something no pig has ever been called before."

"Like what?"

"Oh, I don't know—something elegant. Hyacinth, Guinevere, Ermintrude—that sort of name."

"I'll think about it," said Teresa.

She thought about it over the next week, while the six little Tamworths grew bigger and stronger and began to run around the sty and play games. These mostly took the form of mock fights, and the girl, Teresa noticed, easily held her own against any of her brothers.

She's a real little tomboy, Teresa thought with a mixture of pride and a little regret that

her only daughter was not more ladylike. *I can't possibly give her any of the names Betty suggested. Maybe I should let her choose her own name. I'll ask her.*

"Children!" she called, and when they all came rushing up, she said, "Now you boys go and play quietly in the straw for a little while. I have something to discuss with your sister."

"Tell her not to be so rough, Mom," said one of the little hogs. "She's always beating us up."

"Girls didn't ought to be like that," added another.

"Girls *shouldn't* be like that," said Teresa,

automatically correcting her young son.

"That's right!" they all shouted. "You tell her, Mom!" And off they ran, grumbling.

"Wimps!" said the little gilt scornfully.

"Listen, dear," Teresa began. "I think it's time you had a proper name. It doesn't matter so much with the others. I can just say 'Boys!' if I want to call them. But since you're the only girl, I think it would be nice if you had a name of your own."

"Triffic!" said the little gilt.

"Would you like that?"

"Triffic!"

"Perhaps you'd like to choose your own name," Teresa suggested.

"But, Mom, I don't know any names."

"Well, shall I choose for you?"

"Yes! Triffic!" said the piglet again.

How fond of that word she seems to be, thought Teresa, and then suddenly Betty Berkshire's words came into her mind: "Call her something out of the ordinary, something no pig has ever been called before."

Triffic Tamworth! It had quite a ring to it.

"You've given me an idea," Teresa said, and she shoved her sandy-red snout against her daughter's ear and whispered.

"Weeeee!" squealed the little gilt, and she ran at the biggest of her brothers and sent him flying.

"What are you doing?" he gasped.

"Who do you think you are?" cried the other four hogs.

Loudly and proudly their only sister answered, "I'm Triffic, aren't I, Mom?"

Late that afternoon, the pigman came to give the sows their evening meal. He threw open the gate of Teresa Tamworth's sty—for she was first in line—and, while the piglets played around his feet, he said, as always, "All right, old lady?"

The pigman called all the sows "old lady," whether they were young like Teresa, middle-aged like Betty Berkshire, Sarah Saddleback, Glossy Old-Spots, and Laetitia Large-Black, or actually old like Molly Middle-White.

"I have no idea what you are saying, my good man," grunted Teresa. "And it's a pity you're too stupid to understand me. I could have told you about my daughter's new name."

The pigman poured the food into the trough. Then he checked the piglets, counting

them on the thick fingers of his large hand.

"Only five?" he said. "And all hogs? Oh, no, old lady—don't tell me you've overlaid that little gilt of yours!"

Chapter 2

Octavius

Teresa watched, puzzled, as the pigman ran into the inner part of the sty and searched anxiously through the straw. Counting was not her strong point, and she didn't notice anything amiss until one of the hogs said, "She's gone."

"Who's gone?" asked Teresa.

"What's her name," said another.

"Gone? Where?" asked Teresa.

"Out through the gate," said the third.

"The man left it open," said the fourth hog.

"I hope she never comes back," said the fifth.

"I can't understand it," said the pigman, coming out of the sty again. Then he saw that he had indeed left the gate slightly ajar.

"Little madam!" he cried. "She's run off!" And he hurried out, bolting the gate behind him.

Betty Berkshire's head appeared above the wall.

"What's all the fuss about, dear?" she asked.

"Oh, Betty!" said Teresa. "She's gone!"

"Who?"

"My daughter! My only daughter! She's run away from home. That stupid pigman left the gate open, and she must have slipped out. Oh, dear. Oh, dear. What am I going to do? She's only little, and goodness knows what danger she might run into out there!"

"Calm down, Teresa!" said Betty Berkshire. "As long as she isn't stepped on by a bull or kicked by a horse or squashed by a tractor, she will be quite all right. I'll pass the word along the sties to keep an eye out for her. Have you named her yet?"

"Yes."

"What?"

"Triffic."

"Ah . . . Hmm. Very original," said Betty. "Now you just try to relax, dear. A trouble shared is a trouble halved." And off she went to tell the news to Glossy and Sarah and Laetitia and Molly.

In a short time almost every animal in the Rare Breeds Survival Center had heard, through the grapevine, about Triffic's escape. This rapid spread of information was, as always, thanks to the pigeons. In the middle of the Center's great cobblestone yard— surrounded by the pigsties, the stables, the cattle courts, and the sheep pens—stood an ancient dovecote shaped like a giant pot, in which lived a flock of white fantail pigeons. These birds flew freely around the Center, eating scraps of food left by the other animals and listening with interest to their gossip. One pigeon preening itself on a pigsty wall overheard a conversation between Mrs. Large-Black and old Mrs. Middle-White and flew back to the dovecote to spread the word.

Within half an hour every animal knew that a very small Tamworth piglet by the

name of Triffic was loose, and all eyes were on the lookout for her.

Triffic, however, was nowhere to be seen.

When she first dashed out of the sty, she had run and run as fast as her short legs could carry her. Triffic loved the excitement of being free, with no four walls to enclose her and no five wimpish brothers to annoy her. She had run right across the wide cobblestone yard. It was empty of people, for the day's visitors to the Survival Center had all gone home by that time. On the far side of the yard, she saw an open stable door and hurried inside. She had hardly flopped down on the floor to catch her breath when she heard a voice.

"Go away, rat," the voice said in deep and mournful tones, "or I'll kick your head off."

Triffic looked up to see a tall gray animal standing at the back of the stable with his rump toward her. He was tied to a ring fixed in the wooden feed trough, and he turned his head to look around.

The animal had a bony head with a long nose and floppy splayed ears. The look on his face was gloomy.

Triffic had no idea what kind of animal it was, but she was sure of one thing. "Excuse me," she said, "but I am *not* a rat. I am a pig. And what's more, I am a Rare Breed of pig."

"Oh, spare me all that noise, please," said the tall gray animal. "That's all they talk about in this place nowadays. Pigs, cattle, sheep, goats, chickens, they're all the same—Rare Breed this and Rare Breed that. It makes me sick." He stamped a hind hoof loudly on the floor and pulled a mouthful of hay from the feed trough.

Grumpy old thing, thought Triffic. *He can't be a Rare Breed from the sound of it, but then I don't even know what kind of animal he is. Maybe he's a horse?*

"Are you a horse?" she asked.

"My poor mother was," the gray beast mumbled.

"But you're not?"

"No."

"But if your mother was a horse and your father was a horse, you must be a horse, too."

"My father was a donkey."

"I don't get it," said Triffic.

"I am a mule."

"Oh . . ." said Triffic, still puzzled. "I am a Tamworth," she went on. "My name's Triffic. What's yours?"

The mule swallowed his hay. He turned around as far as his halter would allow, and he looked down at the piglet.

"Octavius," he said.

"What?"

The mule sighed deeply.

"Octavius, young miss," he said, "is my name. And before you ask any more questions, I will tell you that I am the oldest animal in this so-called Rare Breeds Survival Center, which was just an ordinary farm when I was a youngster. Except that the farmer in those days did not care for noisy, smelly tractors. He preferred to work his land with horses and a team of eight mules, of which I was the youngest. That's why I'm called Octavius."

Triffic looked confused.

The mule sighed again.

"I am the sole survivor of that team," he said. "I am very old. I spend a lot of my time alone in this dark stable, alone with my memories of my seven dead friends and of happy days long gone. I have no visitors but the stockman and no company but the rats."

He gave a feeble, husky bray, halfway between a groan and a cough, and his long floppy ears drooped even farther.

"I have no friends," he said.

How miserable he looks, thought Triffic, and quickly she said, "I'll be your friend, Octavius. If you'd like."

At that moment a pigeon landed in the doorway of the stable and waddled up to the piglet, its white tail fanned out behind it.

"Is your name Triffic?" it asked.

"Yes."

"Talk about needles in haystacks," said the pigeon. "We've been looking everywhere for you. Your mother's worried about you. You'd

better go home." And it flew back toward the pigsties to break the news.

Triffic waited a moment for Octavius to respond to her offer of friendship. The old mule said nothing. He merely pulled out another mouthful of hay and munched moodily, his gray back toward her and his tufted tail hanging limp and tired.

"Well, good-bye, Octavius," she said, but still he made no answer, so Triffic scampered back across the yard.

As she neared the line of pigsties, she could see that there were a number of pigeons strutting along the walls, gobbling and cooing. As a result, all her mother's neighbors were standing, resting their feet on their gates and looking out. And as she passed, all of them expressed their opinions of this runaway child. No piglet of theirs, they felt sure, would dream of behaving in such a manner.

"Disgraceful!" grunted Laetitia Large-Black as Triffic passed her sty.

"Scandalous!" sniffed Sarah Saddleback.

"Worrying your poor mother like that!" grumbled Molly Middle-White.

"You should be ashamed of yourself!" growled Glossy Old-Spots.

Betty Berkshire merely snorted, but it was a very expressive snort, and its message was clear.

Only Teresa Tamworth was not on her gate, because the pigman was standing in front of it, looking into the sty.

"Try not to worry, old lady," he was saying as Triffic trotted up behind him. "I've searched everywhere for your little girl, but I can't find her."

And inside, though she didn't understand a word of what he was telling her, Teresa was saying, "I've just heard that my little girl's on her way home, you stupid man. Get off that gate and look behind you."

Which, though her grunts meant nothing to him, the pigman did.

Then he saw Triffic.

He gave a great gasp of relief, opened the door, and let her in.

"Well, well, old lady!" he cried. "What have you got to say about that?"

Teresa Tamworth had a great deal to say.

Like any mother who has been worried

about her child, she felt a mixture of thankfulness and anger. No one listening, as the other sows all were, could have guessed at her delight that her daughter was home safe.

"Naughty, bad, wicked, thoughtless girl!" she stormed. "Only a week old and you go running around anywhere you please instead of staying here with me. Why can't you be good and well behaved like your brothers?"

Triffic did not answer, but the five little hogs looked smug, and the listening sows nodded their heavy heads in approval.

"You are never to run away again," said Teresa. "Do you understand?"

"Yes, Mom," said Triffic.

But don't expect me to stay cooped up in this

boring old sty with my dopey little brothers, she thought. *For one thing, I'm definitely going to see poor old Octavius again. And I've got a lot more exploring to do yet.*

"I won't run away again, Mom," she said.

I'll walk away instead, she thought.

Chapter 3

A Comical Pair

In fact, another whole week passed before Triffic was able to walk away, for the pigman was now very careful about shutting the sty gate at feeding times.

Even then it was a matter of luck.

Each morning, before his breakfast, the manager of the Survival Center liked to wander around and take a look at all the animals before the public was admitted.

As it happened, he arrived at the line of sties as the pigman was cleaning out Teresa Tamworth's. The manager leaned on the outer wall, looking in.

"Everything all right, Joe?" he asked.

"Yes, Boss," said the pigman. "She's taking good care of them."

"Only one gilt, I think you said?"

"Yes, Boss. She's a little madam. Look at her now."

The manager saw the five hogs frisking around their mother as the pigman swept and shoveled with cries of "Move over, old lady!" But the solitary gilt was waiting by the sty gate, peering out through the narrow gap between it and the gate post. She looked alert and tense, like a sprinter waiting at the starting line.

"What's she up to?" asked the manager.

"She wants to run out," said the pigman. "Already did a week ago. I didn't close the gate completely, to tell the truth, and she slipped out. She was gone at least an hour, Lord knows where. I looked all over."

"How did you get her back?"

"She came back on her own," said the pigman. "Little madam." And he disappeared into the inner part of the sty, shovel in hand.

The manager looked over the top of the gate. The piglet stared up at him. The expression in her eyes, he thought, was knowing.

Grinning like a naughty boy, the manager opened the gate a little, expecting the piglet to rush out. He was surprised to see that she walked slowly away up the yard. He bolted the gate again and, following at a distance, saw the piglet disappear into the stable that housed Octavius, the mule.

"Hello, Octavius," said Triffic. "I'm back."

"Yes, I would like that," said Octavius in his gloomy voice.

"Like what?"

"I would like to have you for a friend, young miss," said the old gray mule, continuing their last conversation as if no time had passed, though in fact Triffic had doubled her age since then.

"Oh, great!" said Triffic. "I'll come and visit you often."

"Do they let you out of your sty?" asked Octavius.

"The pigman won't, but just now another man actually opened the gate for me."

"What did he look like?"

"Tall and thin, with a lot of hair on the bottom of his face."

Standing by the stable door, out of their sight but listening, the manager stroked his beard reflectively. He could not, of course, understand a word, but he could hear the piglet's grunting and the soft snickering noises that the mule made in reply. Peering around the opening, he saw that they were almost nose-to-nose, the mule's head bent to the piglet's snout.

I've never seen old Octavius look so relaxed, almost happy, he thought. *Not that he's capable of looking really happy, but he seems to have found a friend at last, grumpy old thing.*

What a comical pair they make! Anyone would think they were talking to each other!

"That must have been the manager who let you out," said Octavius. "The stockman, who looks after me, is a small man with bowlegs."

Even as he said this, a small man appeared at the top of the yard and walked, bowlegged, toward the mule's stable.

"Morning, Boss," he said as he approached. "Just taking Octavius down to the water tank for a drink."

The manager held a finger to his lips.

"Wait a minute, Jim," he said softly. "Take a look in here."

When the stockman saw the odd couple, he took off his greasy old cap and scratched his head.

"Did you ever?" he asked.

They watched in silence for a while.

"I've never known that old mule to allow another animal anywhere near him," said the stockman. "That crabby old cuss would knock the eye out of a fly."

And indeed there was a notice on the stable door that warned of Octavius's bad temper:

OCTAVIUS
Sole survivor of an eight-mule team.
Do not approach this mule
too closely.
He kicks.

But now, when the stockman entered, Octavius did not lay back his long ears or roll his eyes or show his yellow teeth or stamp a warning hoof. He stood, quiet as an old sheep, while the stockman untied his rope and led him out of the stable.

The manager watched as the bony old mule went clip-clopping over the cobbles with the little piglet scuttling along at his heels. At the same time he saw a worried-looking figure come hurrying up the yard. When the pigman caught sight of the odd couple, he took off his greasy old cap and scratched his head.

"Did you ever?" he asked.

At the water tank, Octavius drank deeply. When his thirst was quenched, he bent his gray head to his friend. Drips of water fell from his velvety muzzle onto her upturned snout.

"Here comes the pigman, young miss," he said. "I guess it's time you went back to your mother."

"Okay, Octavius," said Triffic. "See you soon."

"I'll look forward to that," said Octavius, and they touched noses before Triffic turned and trotted on down to the sties, the pigman following.

The manager could see all the sows standing up against their gates, while the fantail pigeons fluttered excitedly about them. He could hear the loud, angry grunting of Teresa Tamworth as she was reunited with her disobedient child.

"Don't be too hard on her, Teresa," he said out loud. "You may be a Rare Breed, but I suspect that piglet of yours is even rarer. She's going to be the star attraction of the Survival Center." And off he went to his breakfast of fried bacon, from an ordinary pig who had not survived.

Chapter 4

Mules Can't

The manager knew that a great many of the visitors to the Survival Center were children, who came either with their parents or in a school group. He also knew that most children love animals, especially a baby animal such as a piglet—and particularly a small sandy-red piglet who, of all the unlikely things, had struck up a friendship with a large gray mule. He had high hopes for Triffic as a crowd pleaser. He needed to make sure lots of people came to the Center so he could get money for his work of saving Rare Breeds.

"Joe," he said to the pigman the next day, "I

want you to let that little Tamworth gilt out every morning, as soon as there are enough visitors around. Do you understand?"

"Yes, Boss," said the pigman, puzzled.

Little madam of a pig, he thought. *What's going on?*

And to the stockman the manager said, "Jim, I want you to exercise Octavius every morning, as soon as there are enough visitors around. Do you understand?"

"Yes, Boss," said the stockman with a frown.

Crabby old cuss of a mule, he thought. *What's going on?*

The sows, too, wondered what was going on.

Gradually, as the days went by, Teresa became used to Triffic's little outings and no longer got angry with her. In fact, she began to feel rather proud that a child of hers should be allowed a privilege that no other piglets had.

But the rest of the sows were none too pleased, especially when they learned from the gossiping pigeons why Triffic was let out.

"She's walking around the yard with a *mule!*" grunted Molly Middle-White.

"A mule!" sniffed Laetitia Large-Black. "The *lowest* form of animal life!"

"And she's attracting *crowds* of people!" grumbled Sarah Saddleback.

41

"People who should be down here admiring *our* children!" growled Glossy Old-Spots.

Even Betty Berkshire, who was friendlier with Teresa than the others were, had to say something. She looked over the wall one day, when the pigman had just let Triffic back into the sty, and shook her head disapprovingly.

"Naughty little girl!" she muttered.

Teresa bristled.

"Are you addressing my daughter, Mrs. Berkshire?" she asked.

"I am," said Betty. "You'll forgive me for saying so, Teresa, but speaking as a much older sow, I think you are allowing the child to make a spectacle of herself."

"You should have heard my mom!" squeaked Triffic to Octavius the next morning. " 'No, Mrs. Berkshire,' she said. 'I will not forgive you, and I'll thank you to mind your own piggishness and keep your snout out of mine.' You should have seen the expression on Auntie Betty's face, Octavius! She was astonished!"

"Your mother sounds like a spirited lady, young miss," said Octavius.

They were walking around the yard

together, the stockman leading the mule and the piglet trotting beside as the crowd of onlookers "oohed" and "aahed" at the sight of the odd couple.

"She is also very lucky," Octavius went on, "to have such a daughter." And he sighed deeply.

"Don't you have a daughter?" asked Triffic.

"No."

"Only sons?"

"No."

"No children at all?"

"No," said Octavius in his usual tones of deepest gloom. "Mules can't."

"Can't have children of their own?" asked Triffic. "Not ever?"

"That's right."

They walked in silence for a while. Then Octavius said, "It never used to bother me, but since meeting you, young miss, I have wished I could have had a child of my own."

Poor old Octavius, thought Triffic, and then she had an idea.

"I'll tell you what," she said. "I haven't got a father—well, I have, but not here. I've never seen him. He lives at another Survival Center.

Mom told me she went there for the wedding. So you could be my adopted father, Octavius. Then you'd have a daughter as well as a friend."

Octavius stopped abruptly in his tracks and stood stock-still. Unbreakably stubborn like all mules, he didn't notice the stockman's efforts to haul him forward again. With a sudden jerk of his head, Octavius twitched the end of the lead rope from the man's hands.

"Young miss," he said, "you have just made an old mule very happy. They named you well when they called you Triffic."

At these words Triffic also felt very happy. Without really thinking what she was doing,

she took the end of the rope in her mouth and walked on. Octavius followed.

"Look at that!" cried somebody in the crowd of watching visitors. Everyone, the children especially, looked and pointed and laughed and cheered at the amazing sight of a very old gray mule being led around the yard of the Survival Center by a very young sandy-red piglet.

The pigman came up to see what all the noise was about and stood beside the stockman.

"Did you ever see such a thing, Jim?" he asked.

"I never did, Joe," said the stockman, and they took off their greasy old caps and scratched their heads.

The next morning the manager, who had been alerted by his men, came to watch.

He stood beside Joe and saw Jim drop the rope. The piglet once again picked up the end of it and walked on. He listened to the delighted comments of the day's visitors.

"What a wonderful pair!" they said.

"It's better than a circus!"

"They should be on TV!"

The manager stroked his beard and smiled behind his hand.

"You know what, Joe?" he said to the pigman. "She's terrific!"

The weeks passed, and more and more people came to visit the Center. In addition to all the Rare Breeds of cattle and horses and sheep and pigs and goats and chickens, they saw the daily show put on in the great yard by old Octavius and his little friend.

And now the act was improved, thanks to an idea of the manager's.

Experimenting with the pair one evening after the people had gone home, he found that when he ordered Octavius to stop, the piglet had to stop, too, since she couldn't pull the mule forward. And when he told Octavius to

go on again, Triffic had to move, or risk being stepped on.

So now, to the visitors' delight, the word "Whoa!" brought the pair to a halt, and they both went forward again at the command "Walk on!"

"What was all that noise I heard just now?" asked Teresa when Triffic returned after the first demonstration of these new skills.

"That was the people, Mom," said Triffic.

"They were cheering for Octavius and me. I don't know why. People are funny creatures. They make a big fuss about nothing, just like my brothers."

She looked around the outer part of the sty.

"By the way, where are they?" she asked. "All asleep inside?"

"No," said Teresa. "They've gone."

"Gone? Where?"

"I don't know," said Teresa (who didn't).

Next door, Betty Berkshire (who did) gave a loud snort. She said nothing, however, since she and Teresa were still not on speaking terms.

The pigman came in with a bucket and filled the trough.

"There you are, old lady, eat up and get your strength back," he said. "We've got to get you in good condition, so you'll be ready for the next litter of piglets. And as for you, little madam," he went on, "you're on your own now. I suppose you'll miss your brothers."

"What's he talking about, Mom?" asked Triffic.

"I haven't a clue," replied Teresa. "I suppose you'll miss your brothers."

"You must be kidding, Mom," said Triffic with her mouth full. "There's no one to hog my food anymore."

Chapter 5

She's Moved In

Leading Octavius around the yard and stopping and starting on command were soon not the only tricks Triffic knew.

All pigs are smart, and Triffic, it seemed, was especially so. She quickly learned a number of other stunts the manager thought up to amuse the visitors.

All of them depended on the cooperation of Octavius. He had always been the most uncooperative animal anyone could imagine, but now, to the stockman's great surprise, he seemed eager to please.

Octavius stood still when told to, and let the

piglet walk between his legs. He lay down flat on his side so she could play King of the Hill on his stomach. He even allowed himself to be harnessed to a kind of sled—on which Triffic had been trained by the manager to stand— and pulled her along behind him. The old mule did all this willingly, with never even the threat of a bite or a kick.

"I can't understand it, Boss," the stockman said. "No one would ever believe what a crabby old cuss he was. He's a changed animal."

The manager nodded. He understood Octavius's improved mood only too well, and he blamed himself fairly and squarely for having allowed the animal to be tied up in a dark stable all this time. At least the manager had now corrected that mistake. He had moved the old mule to a fine roomy box stall. On the door was a new sign that said simply:

OCTAVIUS
The sole survivor of an eight-mule team.

Now, thanks to Triffic, Octavius not only had a friend (*an adopted daughter, you might say,* the manager caught himself thinking with a smile), but also the daily admiration of the crowds who came to watch and applaud the increasingly famous pig-and-mule act. There was such a demand for the pair that they now gave two performances each morning and afternoon.

Triffic worried about this.

"Octavius," she said.

"Yes, my dear."

"Are you sure it's not too much for you? Four shows a day, I mean—all that walking and pulling the sled and everything. You're not as young as you once were, you know."

"On the contrary, my dear girl," replied

Octavius. "I am younger than I was, much younger—in spirit, that is. They feed me better. I even get oats now. I have a large, well-lit new home with room to roll and stretch out in the straw. I have all the fresh air and exercise I lacked before. To be honest, I must confess that I enjoy performing our little shows, as you call them. I like being the center of attention, applauded and cheered by the people. It has made me feel years younger. And it is all thanks to you, my dear."

Triffic was quite reassured by this long speech from her adopted father, which she later reported to her natural mother.

"He's so much happier, Mom," she said. "You wouldn't believe it."

"I am glad for him," said Teresa. "And I am glad for you, child, that you seem to have this gift for spreading happiness. Why, the fantail pigeons tell me you are given a welcome wherever you go in the Center—from the biggest longhorn bull to the smallest bantam hen. Certainly my neighbors have nothing but good things to say about you now."

This change of heart on the part of the other sows was easily explained. Each time

Triffic finished her act and ran home, a great many of the visitors, the children especially, followed her down to the line of pigsties. They paid far more attention than ever before to the rest of the Rare Breed mothers and baby pigs.

"You'd never think they had much in the way of brains," grunted Molly Middle-White, staring up at the people. "But they must—just look at them admiring our children."

"They follow Triffic Tamworth down here, I notice," said Laetitia Large-Black.

"That's true," agreed Sarah Saddleback. "She seems to bring them in this direction."

"At least she's making herself useful," snorted Glossy Old-Spots.

"Maybe we misjudged her," said Betty Berkshire. She looked over the wall and nodded her head approvingly.

"Good little girl!" she said.

"Who, me, Auntie Betty?" asked Triffic.

"Yes, you, dear."

"I'm glad you seem to approve of my daughter now, Betty," said Teresa dryly.

"Oh, yes," Betty replied. "Let bygones be bygones, that's my motto. Life's too short."

For some pigs, anyway, she thought. *Thank goodness I was born a female and of a Rare Breed.*

"I guess it's a relief to be rid of your hogs, Teresa," she said. "A first litter is always tiring. And the way time flies, you'll be hearing the patter of tiny feet again before you know it. You'll want your Triffic out of the way then."

"She's welcome to stay as long as she likes," said Teresa Tamworth.

Triffic saw her chance. For some time now she had been growing tired of having to wait for the pigman to let her out or in. She also hated having to stay in the sty at times when she was not performing. What she wanted was total freedom to go wherever she liked whenever she liked within the Center. She was thinking about sharing Octavius's box stall. The stockman had nailed rails across the front of the stall so the public could lean over them to look at the mule, and Triffic could easily fit underneath them.

"Mom," she said now, "would you mind very much if I moved in with my friend Octavius?"

Teresa hesitated. She was fond of this child, her first and so far only daughter, but she was aware that, as Betty said, there would be other daughters and sons before too long. Besides, some instinct told her that Triffic was a very special pig, destined for great things. After a few minutes, Teresa answered.

"Of course not, my love," she said. "You go and keep your old mule company. But come back to visit now and again, okay?"

"Oh, yes," agreed Betty. "You must come and see us all. You're such a crowd pleaser, you know."

"I will!" Triffic promised. "Every day."

Later, after the second afternoon show, the pigman had finished feeding the sows and was leaning on Teresa's door, waiting for Triffic.

"Where's that little madam gone to now, old lady?" he said when the piglet did not appear, but Teresa only grunted. So the pigman walked up the yard until he saw the stockman coming out of Octavius's box stall.

"Seen my Tamworth gilt, Jim?" he asked.

"You bet I have, Joe," said the stockman,

and he jerked his thumb over his shoulder. "Take a look," he said.

The pigman peered into the stall. There was Octavius, resting comfortably in his deep bed of straw, and beside him lay Triffic.

She jumped up when she saw the pigman and let out a string of little snorts and squeaks that said plainly, "I'm hungry, you stupid man, so please get a trough and some food to put in it, and hurry up about it!"

The pigman obeyed, for even he could not misinterpret this message. Then he and the stockman leaned on the rails, elbows on the upper one, a foot each on the lower, and stared thoughtfully at the odd couple. They did not take off their greasy caps to scratch their heads, because by now they were thoroughly used to the partnership, and the manager had told them how important it had become. Never had the donations been so good, especially since the media had heard about the double act and given the Center extra publicity. Only recently a television crew had come to record the latest trick the manager had taught the pair.

Octavius, harnessed to the sled, was fitted with a set of reins. The manager coated those parts that a human driver would normally have held with molasses. Then he trained Triffic to hold the reins in her mouth. Having a lot of very sweet teeth, she willingly did this, and the nation's TV screens showed the astounding sight of a piglet not merely being pulled along by a mule, but actually driving one.

"I reckon she's moved in, Jim," said the

pigman. "Little madam," he was about to say,
but somehow that no longer seemed right.

"Little marvel!" he said.

"I reckon you're right, Joe," agreed the
stockman. "The old mule will be pleased,
though you'd never think so to look at him."
He was about to add "Crabby old cuss," but
somehow that no longer seemed right.

"Funny old codger!" he said.

The little marvel and the funny old codger
settled down very happily together. Octavius
was never lonely anymore, not for one moment.
Triffic liked to wander all over the Center,

chatting with this animal and that one, and never forgetting regular visits to her mother and her aunties. Her favorite part of the day, however, was the evening. Then she could settle down in the box stall and listen to all the tales Octavius had to tell about the days of long ago.

He spoke of his father, the donkey, and his mother, the mare, and of his seven mates in the eight-mule team. Primus, the eldest, had once been an army mule, carrying heavy machine guns up the mountains in Italy. Quartus and Quintus had worked in a circus. "But the best time, my dear," said Octavius, "was when all eight of us were together, here on the farm. Forget your shire horses and your Percherons and your Suffolk punches—there was no load so heavy that we mules couldn't shift it. What a team we were. They're all gone now though, except me, and I suppose I'll be following them soon."

"Oh, nonsense, Octavius," said Triffic. "There's no danger of that."

But there was.

Late one afternoon, just before closing time—when the last of the day's visitors were leaving the Survival Center—four people were still standing in front of Octavius's box stall. A man and a woman leaned on the top rail, their two children on the bottom, staring at the piglet and the mule.

The children were eating candy, and the man was puffing on a cigarette despite the No Smoking sign on the box stall door—and despite a similar sign on every other door of the Center, where so much hay and straw were stored.

They were not cruel people, just thoughtless. The children tossed their candy wrappers and the bag that had held their

sweets on the floor, despite the fact that a garbage can labeled LITTER stood right beside the stall.

"Time to go," said the man to his wife. He took a final puff, dropped his cigarette butt, and led them all away.

The butt of the cigarette lay on the cobblestones, still glowing. A little breeze blew in through the door and shifted the candy bag toward it. The paper bag caught on fire. It lay burning and might have burned out if the little breeze hadn't blown in once more, lifting and moving the bag just a couple of feet.

But that was enough to drop it onto the edge of Octavius's straw bed.

Chapter 6

A Heroine

Those last four visitors were just walking out of the main gates of the Center as the outer edge of Octavius's bed caught fire.

The pigman was taking a final look down the line of sties, his day's work done. The stockman, in the main stables, was giving a friendly slap to the gleaming black rump of a great shire stallion before leaving.

In his office, the manager stroked his beard contentedly as his secretary told him the total of the day's donations. He converted, in his head, the sum of money into bales of hay and bags of feed for his beloved Rare Breeds.

Octavius was in the middle of a story about Secundus, the strongest mule of the team. He had once been hitched to a cow that had slipped into a deep ditch and had hauled her out all by himself.

At that moment the burning candy bag caught onto the thick dry straw and rose in an almost solid wall of flame along the rails across the front of the box stall.

"Quick!" groaned the old gray mule, backing hastily away from the blaze. "Get out while you can!"

Triffic dashed to safety beneath the far end of the bottom rail, where the flames had not yet reached. She turned to see them take hold there, too. There was a side door to the box stall, she knew, but it was bolted. Octavius was too big to get under or between the rails and too old and stiff to be able to jump out.

The first thought Triffic had was to get help. The last thing she heard, as she ran squealing at the top of her voice down the yard, was the frantic battering of Octavius's heels as he tried to kick down the rails.

The pigman heard the earsplitting nonstop noise the piglet was making and looked up

and saw the smoke. He grabbed a couple of buckets and ran for the water tank as fast as he could.

The stockman, too, heard the noise and saw the smoke. He unreeled the stable hose and ran for the box stall as fast as his bowlegs would let him.

Both men yelled, "Fire! Fire!" and the manager heard them from his office.

"Call 9–1–1! Quick!" he snapped at his secretary, and he snatched a fire extinguisher off the wall.

He could hear the crackle of flames as he raced across the yard, and because he was in good shape and long-legged, he arrived at the same time as his men. Flinging them the extinguisher, he dashed around to the side door of the box stall.

Triffic watched all this, her heart thudding madly. There was no sound from within now, nothing but the roar of the fire. A trapped horse would have been screaming, but a mule will bear terrible pain and make no sound. Triffic did not know this. *He's dead,* she said to herself.

Then, as the manager threw back the bolt

of the side door, to her immense relief, she saw Octavius totter out. He was shaking like a leaf, she could see, and the tuft on the end of his tail had been scorched off, but he was safe!

By the time the fire engine arrived, the three men had the fire under control. All that remained was for the firemen to use their hoses on neighboring buildings to wet them down.

Things could have been much worse.

The rails had burned, and the wooden trough, too. Octavius's tack, hanging on the blackened wall, was ruined. But the roof was undamaged, and everything could be repaired.

Only the manager noticed that by a strange chance the flames that had licked at the sign on the stall door had been selective. Now it simply read:

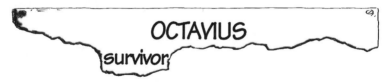

"Things could have been much worse," he said to Joe and Jim, when the firemen had left.

"We'd have been too late, Boss," the

stockman said, "if it hadn't been for Joe's little Tamworth."

"Jim's right," agreed the pigman. "If she hadn't made all that noise, we'd never have noticed in time. She saved the old mule's life."

"And a lot more lives, too," said the manager, brushing bits of blackened straw out of his beard. "If that fire had really taken hold, it would have run right down the line of buildings, Dutch barn and all. The Center would have been pretty much ruined. That piglet's a heroine, and I'll make sure the newspapers hear all about it. Just look at the pair of them now."

The three men looked down the yard, where Octavius, still trembling, was taking a long drink. Then, his thirst quenched, he bent his gray head to his friend, while drips of water fell from his velvety muzzle onto her upturned snout.

"Thank you, my dear little girl," he said simply, and they rubbed noses.

Some weeks passed before Triffic and Octavius could put on their act again. The old mule needed a rest to recover from the shock, the manager thought. Besides, the tack and

the sled, which had also burned, had to be replaced.

Meanwhile the box stall had to be repaired and thoroughly cleaned, the walls painted, and the rails and trough replaced.

No one knew for sure what had caused the fire, but there was little doubt in the manager's mind. He had a large new sign made and posted by the main gates. It said:

> **SMOKING is strictly prohibited anywhere in the Center.**
> **Your carelessly dropped cigarette butts could cost the lives of these animals.**
> **We want our Rare Breeds to survive.**
> **PLEASE DO NOT SMOKE.**

Everyone knew, from the newspapers and television, of the fire and of the heroic part the piglet had played (as indeed did all the animals in the Center, for the pigeons told them). Everyone was waiting eagerly to see the odd couple perform once again. But in the meantime, something else happened.

Triffic went down to the pigsties one morning to say hello to her mother and was surprised to find a crowd of people gathered around the Tamworth's sty.

There was nothing unusual about the sows attracting attention—lots of people came to admire old Molly with her squashed-in face, or the gleaming blackness of Laetitia or Sarah's saddle or Glossy's spots, or dark brown Betty Berkshire with her white forehead and feet and her double chin. But why, this day, was everyone pushing and shoving to look into the sty of sandy-red, long-snouted Teresa Tamworth?

Triffic stood behind the feet of the jostling crowd, wondering what could possibly be happening.

Just then two fantails flew down from the old dovecote and began to peck around at bits of food that people had dropped.

"What's up?" asked Triffic. "Is my mom all right?"

"She's all right, there's no doubt about that," said one of the pigeons.

"Haven't you heard?" said the second pigeon.

"No, what?"

"Happy event," said the first bird.

"Seven happy events," corrected the other.

"Two boys . . ."

". . . and five girls."

Triffic ran to find Octavius.

"You'll never guess what's happened!" she squealed excitedly. "I've got two brothers and *five* sisters! Oh, Octavius, Mom must be so pleased!"

That evening, when all the visitors had gone, Triffic went across the yard again and stood outside her mother's door.

"Mom!" she called.

"What is it, dear?" asked Teresa. "I'm rather busy."

"But, Mom, can't I see the new babies?"

"Not just now."

"Later then?"

"We'll see."

"Be a good girl and run along, Triffic," said Betty Berkshire from next door. "Your mother doesn't want to be bothered."

"Mom doesn't want to be bothered with me anymore, Octavius," wailed Triffic that night.

"It's natural," said Octavius. "All her concern is for her new litter." He gave his feeble bray, half cough, half groan.

"You mustn't be sad about it," he said, "or you'll make me feel sad again, and that will never do."

"It certainly won't," agreed Triffic.

She looked at her friend's face, set as usual in an expression of extreme melancholy.

"You are happy, Octavius, aren't you?" she asked.

"I am, my dear," said the old mule. "As long as I have you."

And he was even happier a couple of days later when they moved back into the renovated box stall. New tack had been bought, and a new sled made. Then, after a period of rehearsals, they were ready for the first performance since the fire.

The pigman had groomed Triffic with great care, oiling her sandy-red hair and even cleaning and polishing her feet.

As for Octavius, the stockman had brushed and currycombed him till his gray coat shone. His long ears, as usual, would not stand up properly. His upright mane was too short to do

much with, and the hair on his tail tassel had not yet fully grown back. But he looked in fine shape for such an old fellow, all the same. It was hard to remember now that bony, mournful-looking wreck upon which Triffic Tamworth had first set eyes.

What a crowd turned out that morning! The great cobblestone yard of the Survival Center was packed with people applauding and cheering as Triffic and Octavius went through their act.

The manager stood watching the finale—Triffic driving Octavius, the molasses-smeared reins held in her mouth. Then, as the sled came to a stop, Triffic jumped off, got down on her knees, and bowed to the crowd.

She performed the new trick perfectly, and the manager stroked his beard and listened to the roars of applause.

Just in front of him a small boy was jumping up and down and shouting with excitement.

"Did you enjoy it?" asked the manager.

"Yes!" cried the boy. "It's great! What's his name, mister?"

"Octavius," he replied.

"That's a funny name."

"Well, you see, he's the survivor of an eight-mule team."

"No," said the boy. "I don't mean the mule. I mean the pig. What's his name?"

"It isn't a he," said the manager. "It's a she. And actually, she hasn't got a name."

"She's triffic!" said the boy. "That's what she is!"

"Okay," said the manager. "You said it. She's Triffic."